Where's that sunbeam going?

HEY!

SUNBEAM!
GET BACK HERE!

Great.

Now I'm wide awake, and I only got nineteen hours of sleep.

Sigh.

CAT PROBLEMS

by Jory John
illustrated by Lane Smith

WALKER BOOKS
AND SUBSIDIARIES

LONDON • BOSTON • SYDNEY • AUCKLAND

To William, Olive, Ferris Mewler, Kurt, and Zoe.
—J.J.

To A.J., Noodle, Pretzel, Wizzy, and Lulu.
—L.S.

First published in Great Britain 2021 by Walker Books Ltd
87 Vauxhall Walk, London SE11 5HJ

10 9 8 7 6 5 4 3 2 1

Text © 2021 Jory John
Illustrations © 2021 Lane Smith

The right of Jory John and Lane Smith to be identified as author and illustrator respectively of this work has been asserted by them in accordance with the Copyright, Designs and Patents Act 1988

Published by arrangement with Random House Children's Books, a division of Penguin Random House LLC, New York, U.S.A.

This book has been typeset in Georgia

Printed in China

British Library Cataloguing in Publication Data: a catalogue record for this book is available from the British Library

ISBN 978-1-5295-0613-6

www.walker.co.uk

Book design by Molly Leach

Ahem.

You're in my spot.

That's where I curl up,
sometimes.

Now you're in my
other spot.

Now you're in my **_third_** spot.

I think that cat might be my greatest enemy in the entire house.

My paws are dirty.

Blech.

I guess it's time for my
seventeenth bath of the week.

A little privacy, *please.*

Hey, look,

an empty box.

Now what?

My eyelids are getting heavy ...

heavier ...

heaviest...

THUMP!

VROOOOOOM!

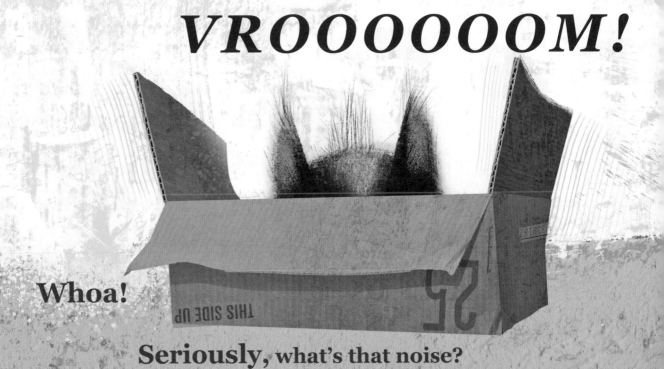

Whoa!

Seriously, what's that noise?

Now what?

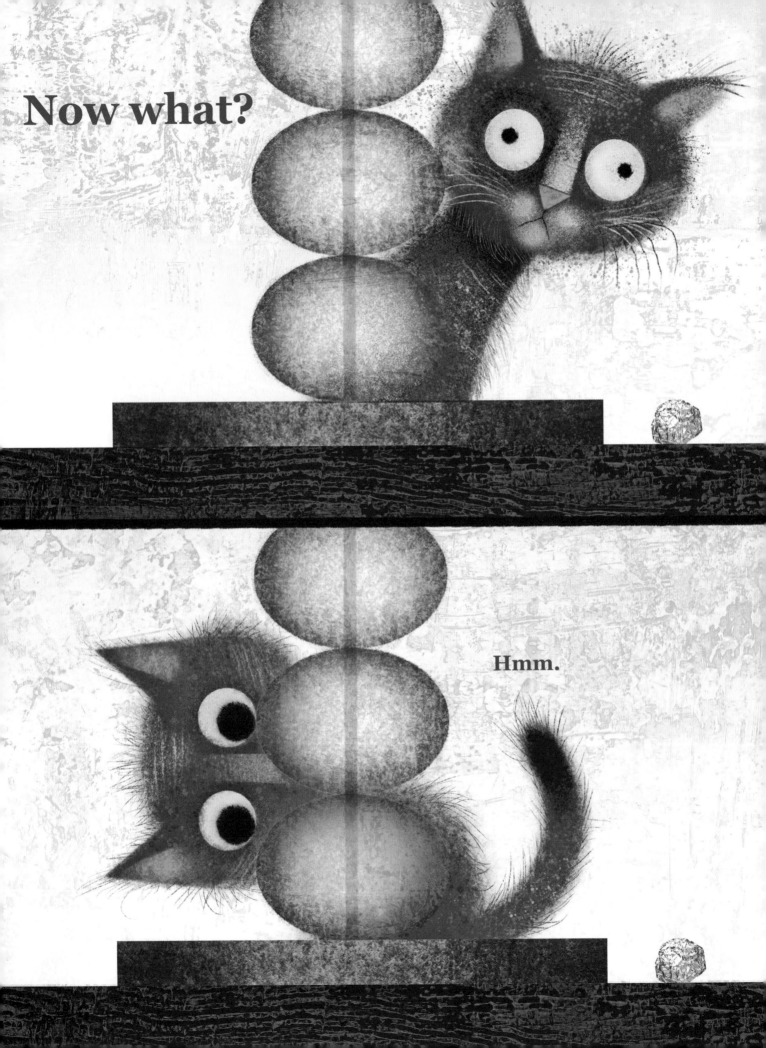

Hmm.

I guess I'll bat this piece of foil around.

bat bat bat

I think that monster's gone.

For now.

I need to know what's going
on in every room of this place.

I want to eat
that plant.

I want
to chomp
that book.

I want to scratch the sofa, but
I already tore all the material
off both arms.

I want to rip
that curtain.

But hey, that's just me.

You're in my spot. Again.

You're in my *other* spot.

You're in my spot. Again.

You're in my *other* spot.

Why am I even *standing* here?

Like, this is pretty random, even for *me*.

Wait, why did I just sniff that catnip toy?

Sheesh.
Now I'll be awake all night!
Goodness gracious.

Why can't I stop smelling this shoe?
I have to stop.
Still ... it's intriguing.

What is it about this shoe?

Is this what the
OUTSIDE
smells like?

Things would be
different if I knew
how to open a door.

I haven't been outside in eight years.

Sigh.

I'm trapped in this *house* all the time.

I just go from room to room with nothing to *do*!

You! Cat! Hello!

I confess that I have watched you mope

Now listen to me, Cat: Somebody feeds you.

Somebody gives you water.

you warm and even hands you treats.

around outside, hiding nuts that I'll never again locate,

Things are difficult out here, Cat.

This tree, although it's shared with roommates.

which I'm saving for some reason. A button.

Sure, you may be housebound, and you may

current living situation, but look at *me*, Kitty.

OUTSIDE? **Honestly**, what I

a *touch* of boredom from time to time. **Yes,**

paw to trade places with you for a day.

And start embracing the life you have.

will fall into place after that.

Think about

I spy you through this window.

around your house for *months*.

Somebody changes your litter box.

Somebody brushes you and keeps

Treats, I say! Meanwhile, I scurry

evading predators that only seem to multiply.

I don't have much. My branch, of course.

A few nuts I've kept. A piece of ribbon,

And that's about it.

find reasons to gripe about your

You think it's so great

wouldn't give for just

I would give my right

So quit saying, "Poor me."

Everything else

it...

How can I eat this very talkative squirrel?

Hmm.

He's lucky there's this window screen separating us.

Things would be different if I knew how to open window screens.

I have nothing to do, and I'm vaguely hungry.

Maybe I'll miaow for a while.

Let's see how this plays out...

Mraowww! Mraowww! Mraowww!
Mraowww! Mraowww! Mraowww!
Mraowww! Mraowww! Mraowww!
Mraowww! Mraowww! Mraowww!
Mraowww! Mraowww! Mraowww!
Mraowww! Mraowww! Mraowww!
Mraowww! Mraowww! Mraowww!
Mraowww! Mraowww! Mraowww!
Mraowww! Mraowww! Mraowww!
Mraowww! Mraowww! Mraowww!

Let's try this again...

Mraowww! Mraowww! Mraowww!
Mraowww! Mraowww! Mraowww!
Mraowww! Mraowww! Mraowww!
Mraowww! Mraowww! Mraowww!
Mraowww! Mraowww! Mraowww!
Mraowww! Mraowww! Mraowww!
Mraowww! Mraowww! Mraowww!
Mraowww! Mraowww! Mraowww!
Mraowww! Mraowww! Mraowww!
Mraowww! Mraowww! Mraowww!
Mraowww! Mraowww! Mraowww!
Mraowww! Mraowww! Mraowww!
Mraowww! Mraowww! Mraowww!
Mraowww! Mraowww! Mraowww!
Mraowww! Mraowww! Mraowww!
Mraowww! Mraowww! Mraowww!

Yessssss!
My whole day has led me to this wet food.
This is a highlight, for sure.
And that says quite a lot about my day.

I guess it's OK in here.

Sometimes.

munch, munch, munch

Yum.
That's not bad.
Not bad at all.

I already want some more.

Mraow? Anyone? Mraowww?

Hmm.

Now what?

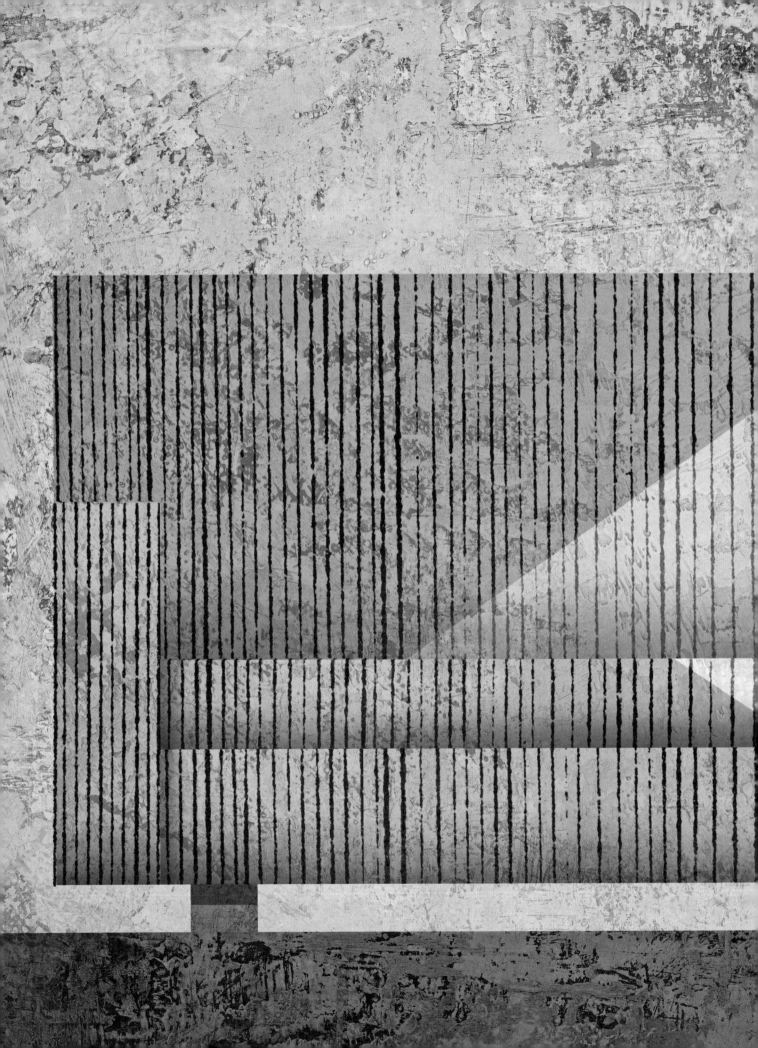

You're in my spot.

When's that sunbeam coming back?